Our World Has Changed But YOU Stayed the Same

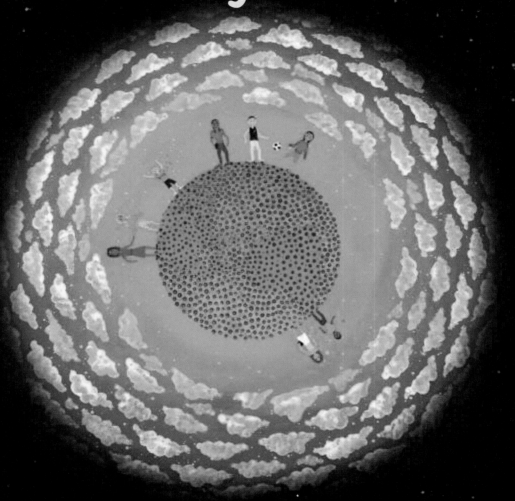

Yvonne Elliott

This book is dedicated to my two amazing children, Monterey and Landon. Your resilience, kind-heartedness, loving, caring, empathetic hearts make me so proud to be your mom. You are the lights and loves of my life. Thank you for the constant reminder to never give up hope, always follow your dreams and to inspire others, while also making a difference in the lives of others every single day! I love you both to the moon and back!

Love,

Mommy (your best friend for life)

There is a virus, they said on T.V. Everyone stopped what they were doing . . . But YOU did not.

You stayed the same. You played outside with your friends, laughing and smiling. You baked cookies with your mom and played games with your dad.

School is cancelled, they said. Each day was now very different. No morning alarms, no school bells, no classmates or sweet teachers welcoming you into the classroom.

The world had changed . . . But YOU stayed the same.

You woke up happy, had pancakes for breakfast, giggled with your siblings and played with your pets.

Everything changed . . . But YOU stayed the same.

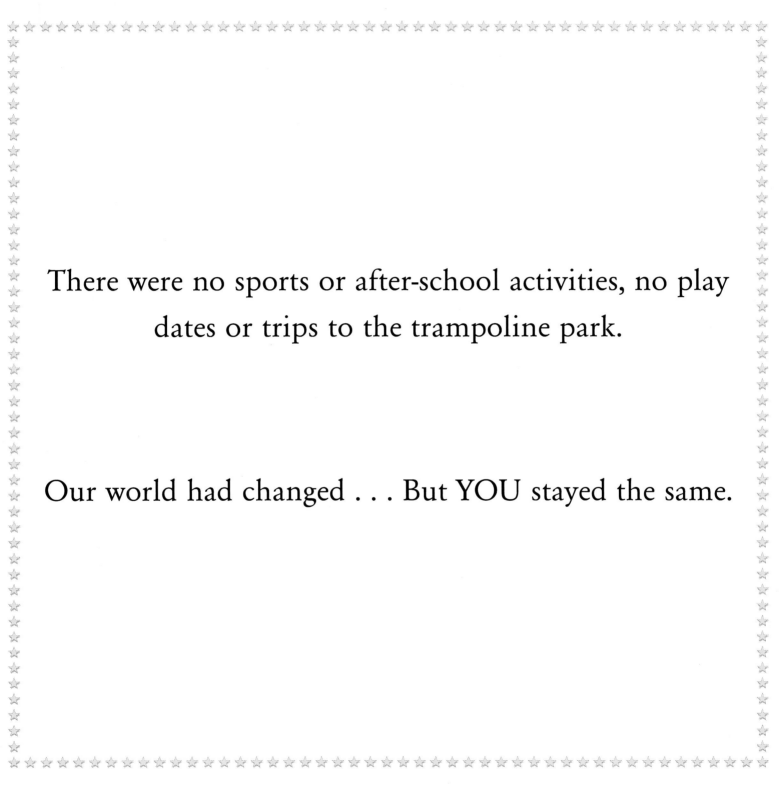

There were no sports or after-school activities, no play dates or trips to the trampoline park.

Our world had changed . . . But YOU stayed the same.

You read books, watched movies, told funny jokes and had so many snuggles with your family.

You loved, you hugged, your helped, you cared . . .

Everything had changed But YOU stayed the same.

Instead of school, there were zoom calls and more time spent at home.

Instead of visiting family and friends, there was Face Time, phone calls and cards.

The world was so different . . . But YOU stayed the same.

You made your grandparents smile, you worked hard
on your school work.

You still loved and cared with all your heart.

You danced to music, sang along to your favorite songs and watched virtual concerts.

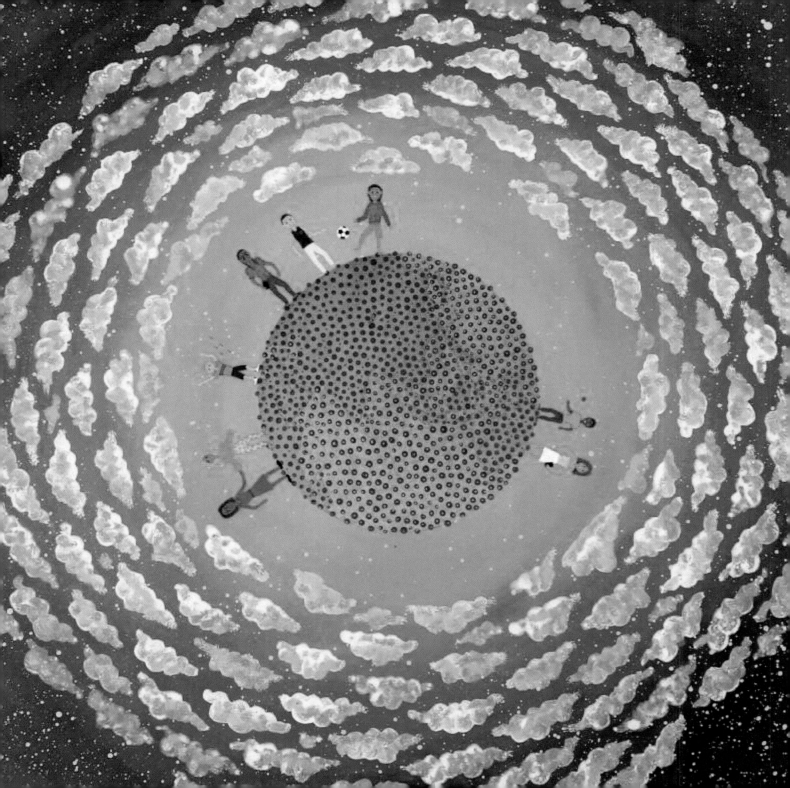

It was all so very DIFFERENT . . .

Yet YOU stayed the same!

Made in the USA
Columbia, SC
04 March 2021